# Over at the Rink

# Over at the Rink

## A Hockey Counting Book

**Stella Partheniou Grasso**
illustrated by **Scot Ritchie**

Scholastic Canada Ltd.
Toronto  New York  London  Auckland  Sydney
Mexico City  New Delhi  Hong Kong  Buenos Aires

Scholastic Canada Ltd.
604 King Street West, Toronto, Ontario M5V 1E1, Canada

Scholastic Inc.
557 Broadway, New York, NY 10012, USA

Scholastic Australia Pty Limited
PO Box 579, Gosford, NSW 2250, Australia

Scholastic New Zealand Limited
Private Bag 94407, Botany, Manukau 2163, New Zealand

Scholastic Children's Books
Euston House, 24 Eversholt Street, London NW1 1DB, UK

The art for this book was created using pencil and ink.
This was scanned into the computer where all the colouring was done.

Library and Archives Canada Cataloguing in Publication
Partheniou Grasso, Stella
Over at the rink / by Stella Partheniou Grasso ; illustrations by Scot Ritchie.

Based on the rhythm of the traditional counting rhyme, Over in the meadow.
ISBN 978-1-4431-1374-8

1. Counting-out rhymes. 2. Hockey--Juvenile poetry.
I. Ritchie, Scot II. Title.

PS8631.A787O94 2012          jC811'.6          C2012-901660-8

6  5  4  3  2  1      Printed in Singapore  46      12  13  14  15  16

*To Lenny; my hat's off to you, Captain.*
— S. P. G.

*To my wonderful, hockey loving brother, Flyn.*
— S. R.

Over at the rink
Where the anthem's sung,
The whole town gathered
For some hockey fun . . .

2

Over at the rink
Beneath the winter sun,
Were the two linesmen
And the referee one.

4

"Be fair!" called the linesmen.
"I'm fair!" called the one.
So they all blew their whistles
And the game had begun.

Over at the rink
From behind the line of blue,
Stood our eagle-eyed goalie
And defencemen two.

6

"Block!" cried the goalie.
"We'll block!" cried the two.
So they guarded and they blocked
As defencemen do.

7

Over at the rink
While the puck zoomed free,
Our mascot cheered
To the forwards three.

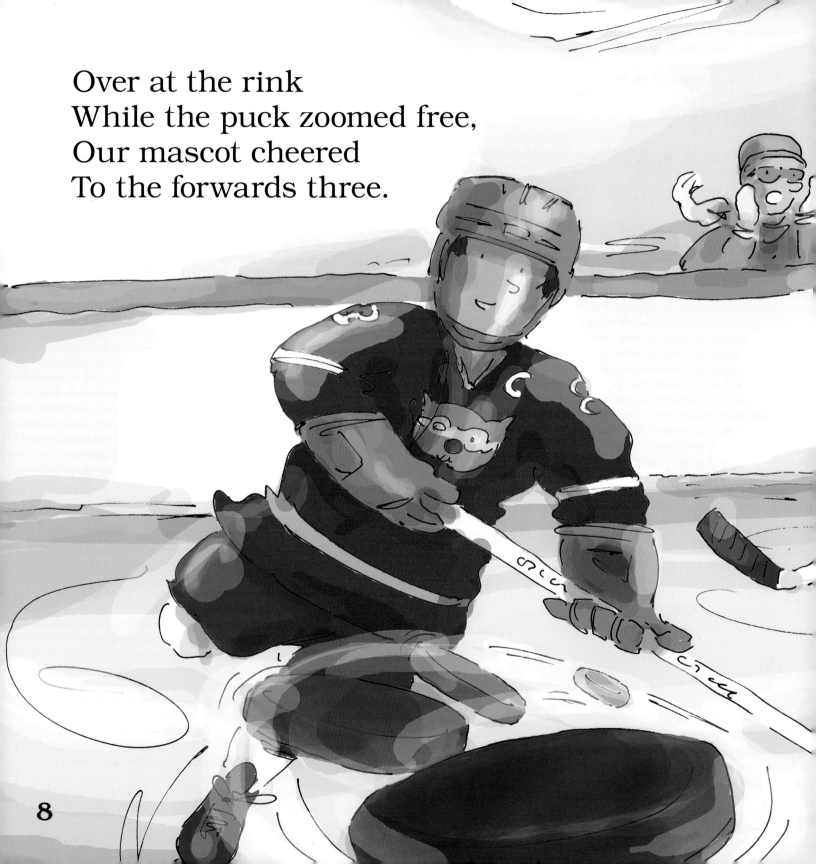

8

"Skate!" cheered the mascot.
"We'll skate!" cheered the three.
So they skated and they passed
While the puck zoomed free.

9

Over at the rink
When the visitors scored,
Our head coach planned
With his helpers four.

"Time!" barked the coach.
"Time out!" barked the four.
So they worked out a play
When the visitors scored.

Over at the rink
Where the air was alive,
Our captain rallied
His players five.

"Win!" roared the captain.
"We'll win!" roared the five.
So they pushed for the win
And the air was alive.

Over at the rink
Through a maze of sticks,
McNevin drove a shot
Past the visitors six.

"In!" sang McNevin.
"It's in!" groaned the six.
And we tied up the score
Through a maze of sticks.

Over at the rink
With their eyes on McNevin,
Were a sharp talent scout
And reporters seven.

16

"Goal!" raved the scout.
"What a goal!" raved the seven.
They were glued to the game
With their eyes on McNevin.

Over at the rink
As the players did skate,
The biggest fan stood
With his best buddies eight.

18

"Go!" yelled the fan.
"Way to go!" yelled the eight.
And they cheered for their heroes
As the players did skate.

19

Over at the rink
As the clock ran out of time,
Our head coach called
To player number nine.

"Fly!" said the coach.
"I'll fly!" said number nine.
And he darted and he deked
As the clock ran out of time.

Over at the rink
Nine scored for the win!
The whole crowd cheered
With the old-timers ten.
"Great!" hailed the crowd.
"Great game!" hailed the ten.
While the players all hollered . . .

"Let's play again!"

Over at the rink
Another game's done.
Everybody to the ice
For some skating fun!

26

27